Lunar series book 3: King's Fo

Other series by Whittney Corum

Lunar series
Mix Blood
False Trails

Simple heart series
Simple Heart

Memories of Saga Series
Child of Forest and Ice
Son of Night, King of Shadows

Whittney Corum

Chapter 1... 5
Chapter 2... 12
Chapter 3... 19
Chapter 4... 25
Chapter 5... 31
Chapter 6... 38
Chapter 7... 41
Chapter 8... 47
Chapter 9... 54
Chapter 10... 63
Chapter 11... 70
Chapter 12... 78
Chapter 13... 84
Chapter 14... 93
Chapter 15... 98
Chapter 16... 108
Chapter 17... 115
Chapter 18... 120
Chapter 19... 126
Chapter 20... 133
Chapter 21... 144
Chapter 22... 152
Chapter 23... 160
Chapter 24... 164
Chapter 25... 169
Chapter 26... 175

Lunar Series Book 3:

King's Folly

by

Whittney Corum

Whittney Corum

Copyright@2023 by Whittney Corum.

All rights reserved. No part of this book may be reproduced, scanned,

or distributed in any printed or electronic form without permission.

Lunar series book 3: King's Folly

Chapter 1
Astrid

What do you tell someone when they are at their wit's end? How do you guide someone lost in pain and confusion? How do you tell someone that you are at the end of your rope?

Well, the answer is simple for a dragon: fly. It appears to be a good idea, but when the said dragon is only a few months old and hasn't even learned to fly yet, it's something else.

"No, Almond, it's not time to fly," I told my 5-month-old fledgling.

Almond just huffed, blowing little puffs of smoke. I frowned; out of all my children, Almond had to be the most stubborn, so instead of holding my beautiful baby boy, I watched a dark purple and green fledgling run around the nursery cave, trying to fly.

"Almond, I will not tell you again." I threatened.

My boy, my flesh and blood which I carried, just huffed and started to jump only to be caught by his sire. I sighed in relief at the reddish-black head and mismatched eyes that held the fledgling.

"I heard you might need help." my mate said, a slight smirk on his face.

"I believe this one has taken more after you than me."

"I seemed to recall a Shifter mix who was told to stay away from the Dance of Flares and came anyway."

"I had to," I whispered as a wave of sadness washed over me.

"Astrid." I heard my mate say.

"I'm fine; it all turned out for the best."

"I often wonder that." I hear him mutter under his breath.

"Blaggdon?" I asked.

"It's nothing; it's time for this one to be put to bed."

"Alright."

"I'll do it; you need some rest."

I sighed, watching the two of them go; as they did, my mind went to memories I hid deep in my heart. The day I saved the babe, Adian, and fell in love with Keyne, his Dragon father. Falling in love with the said dragon and forced to leave by him.

Then, I found myself on an adventure to save my love and his kind. Only to be chained and forced to wed a fake. Watched as my love bled from wounds, and only to find him again, but merged with another by magic only known to dragons. It saved both their lives, and I don't blame either one.

Yet, it seemed after the birth of our twins and the death of one of the council members, my mate seemed more distant. I know it's partly my fault for the death since my sister, in her love for me, chose the misguided step of bringing dragon hunters to the heart of dragon territory, and my messenger, whom I had trusted, had betrayed me to get back an ancient goddess who almost destroyed the world.

We did stop it, though, like the fallen knight and queen before. The duo had tried to take control of the dragons to cause a war. They also wanted to kill me but were punished by the god Flickron.

Yet after that battle, we became closer, and the twins were the gift of that closeness. This time, though, as we healed from the wounds of the body and mind, it seemed our hearts were taking longer.

"I think I'll head to the bath."

He gave a slight nod as he gently rocked our child. I held back an urge to say something more, but my voice was weighed down by tiredness and worry. I left the room, my footsteps silent from years of hunting with my papa and uncle.

The bath was in one of the most immense caverns in our dragon lair. It was a cavern filled with a pool of water that was so clear you could see to the bottom. It was lighted by fire stones, which had a faint glow to bring comfort and light to the space.

I was about to undress when I heard a rustle behind me. I sighed, turning around to see a figure dressed in trader's garb with winter blond hair and hand fox-golden eyes. Flickron stood before me, the God of tricksters, travelers, performers, and my birth father.

"Flick, I'm fine. I'm just a little tired."

"I wish I were here about your health," he said, his eyes dancing with anger and sadness.

"What's the matter?"

"The king of the Zodiac is dead, and with that, all the lives of elves, shifters, and dragons, along with others, are forfeit in the land of Kardian."

Chapter 2
Emyr

I never felt as helpless as when my father gave his last breath. It was as if his last breath brought death not just to him but to his ideas. I wanted to reach out to stop it, the death of not just my father but the destruction of races that would be lost because of my brother's rage.

"Rian, please." my voice called to him, but like a wave hitting a rock, it bounced back and answered with a voice burning with pain.

"Don't plead for them, Emyr, the beasts who have no cause for our mercy or time. It's their fault our father is dead."

"Our father died because it was his time.." I said before wincing as the sound of porcelain fell to the stone floor.

"Don't speak of his time when our father didn't even get to see his grandchildren, while the Elf king has seen more than three generations of his offspring and grandchildren. Shifters see their clans grow in their old age, and dragons live hundreds of years to see their line."

My brother's body shook with each word as if the words were shaking him to his core. His dark blue eyes burned with the flames of the sun. His nails cut into his palms, almost causing them to bleed.

"I.."

"My king." the sweet nectar voice of my sister-in-law floated through the air.

Calista is the daughter of the Southern Islands. A beauty blessed by Solara herself with raven locks and skin kissed by the goddess. Her eyes were dark as sweet chocolate but with hints of gold. Yet, with all her beauty and grace, I couldn't help but see darkness underneath.

A woman who wanted the elves, beings made from starlight by the Lady of Lace, gone because of their beauty. She wanted dragons because of the hoards of gold that were rumored to have. Yet out of all of them, she hated the shifters, the creatures who could change their form at will. I didn't know for sure, but I had heard whispers of her brother being killed because his wife loved a shifter.

I didn't understand why my father had agreed for her to marry my brother. My brother's hate had been known to everyone in the palace. I did ask him once, but my father just shook his head.

"When you get older, you will know that sometimes one's hate can be broken when faced with the same hatred."

"My heart, what are you doing here?"

"I wanted to see you. Since father took his last breath, I thought you could use comfort," she replied, her arms intertangling around my brother's neck.

"You are, Emyr was just leaving."

I looked at my brother, feeling my anger filling my mind. I opened my mouth to say something when another set of footsteps entered the room.

My eyes fell on Willow, my aid and friend. Yet, as he came to me, I could see his eyes flash with fear at the couple before us. Yet it was gone when he looked over at me.

"Willow?"

"My prince, High Priest Ango, needs to meet with you."

"The voice of Solara? Why would he want to talk to Emyr instead of the king?" Calista asked, her voice singing.

"Leave it alone, dear; you forget Emyr is a novice of Solara. It is quiet time for him to return to the fold." my brother said, eyes on me.

I simply bowed to get Willow away from the hatred in the couple's eyes. Even though Willow's father was human, the two could see the golden hair of elves in the locks of brown he bore. I quickly left with him right beside me.

"So what does master want with me."

"Forgive me, my prince, but I lied," Willow said, bowing.

"What.."

"Ango didn't send for you, child of Solara; I did." a voice of soft winds echoed in my ear.

I turned to see a woman dressed in white lace, pale moon hair tied back with a strand of gold and black mixed into it. Willow bowed and followed suit, even though she wasn't my goddess.

"Lady of Lace."

"Rise, Emyr, for I need your strength."

"For what?"

"To save the land and people who live in it."

Chapter 3
Blaggdon

Peace is a feeling of ease for everyone and everything in a moment. Peace when you are with the ones you love, knowing that they are safe. Peace when the cool quiet of the day melts into a night with your Flarea holding her close as the moon and stars dance around you.

Peace that even if you were to leave, your family could continue. I need to know that, both parts of me.

I heard from him as I put my son to bed, smiling at the soft coo. I then walked over to check on his sister—the reddish-black locks grow in simple curls. Asling was the quietest of my children, and she loved to watch the world around her. I kissed her curls before heading to the room which housed our eldest son.

Aiden was now 4 with locks of golden hair. He had lost some of his smiles when he lost his uncle to betrayal but had gotten it back when he saw his siblings. He is a kind child and loves to help both his mother and me.

"You will be a great king," I whispered before wincing in pain.

I quickly left the room to the hallway, one hand on the stone and the other on my heart. Pain came from it, and I could hear a whisper echoing in my ear. A voice telling me soon it would be time to pay.

"Not now. Just a little more time." I pleaded to the wind, growling a little in pain.

"You aren't the first to ask that dragon."

The hallway was gone, leaving a black space. In front of me was a figure dressed in silver and black, his ink-black hair falling to his shoulders. Skin as pale as death and eyes pitch black with hints of grey and gold.

"Erembour, god of death," I said, taking a breath.

"Yes, and you are the breath of both Bragdon and Kyene. A life saved by magic that wasn't supposed to be used and came with a price."

"I know…but it was the only way to protect her."

"I understand that. Even I who embraces death still knows the joy of love, but also the sting of knowing that I can't protect her from everything."

"Then what must I do to make sure they are all safe? I need more time…"

"Time, I'm afraid I can't give you, for it's not just me but fate that holds your life. Your life is in the hands of fate, and I can't stop it. But I can give you a gift."

"A gift? What gift would the king of death give me?" I asked venom in my voice.

"Be careful; you might be the Dragen, but you are still mortal," his voice echoed, forcing me to the floor.

"I'm sorry," I said, looking down.

"I know; I have seen mortals who fight tooth and claw to stay from me. Some use tricks that their blood gives, those that have one thing in common. The trickster." I could hear a slight growl in his voice.

"Flickron…"

"I'm not going to talk about your Flarea's birth father. I'm here to warn you of the bloodshed of dragons, Flare and Flarea, elves, and shifters."

"A war."

"The king of Zodiac has entered my embrace, and his eldest son and wife want all creatures that don't embrace Solara to be wiped from this world."

"How do I stop this?"

"You can't, at least not in a way I can see. I give this warning so the innocent can be protected, those who can't fight."

"Why help us at all?"

Whittney Corum

"Because even the God of death doesn't want to see young in their presence."

Chapter 4
Astrid

After the talk with Flickron, my feet flew against the stones. My only thoughts were getting to my mate and telling him the news. I was entering a hallway when I saw my mate's hand on the wall.

"Blaggdon?" I called, my heart beating fast in fear and worry.

"Flarea." I thought I heard him gasp as he turned to me.

Strong arms went around me, holding me tight. It was as if my mate was trying to keep me from leaving. If he let go, I would disappear. I could hear his heartbeat, a drum that had lost its beat in chaos.

"I'm here, my love," I replied, trying to ground him.

In a few moments, he took a deep breath. His heart steadied as he pulled slightly away. I felt a brush of his lips against mine before he stepped back. As he did, my mind screamed for him to stay, as if he had stepped away and we were dividing ourselves.

"I just had a visit from the King of Death," he said, his voice leveled with venom.

"Erembour? Why would he come here? Flickron can come and go as he pleases, but isn't the king of death bound to his home?"

"I don't know, but he had a message for me," he replied, looking away.

"What was it?" I asked, reaching out to touch his cheek.

He caught my hand as if he didn't want me to feel him. Blaggdon, realizing what happened, sighed and kissed my hand, giving a gentle smile as if to comfort me. I bit my lip, and he sighed before kissing my head.

"Just know that our children and you will be safe."

"It's war, then," I replied, my body shaking.

"War, and as the Dragen, I must ensure my people are safe, including you."

"I'm your mate, I need to…"

"You need to protect our children, and as the Flare of the Dragen, you must be able to lead our people to safety."

"If the prince wants us all dead, then is a place safe for us here?" I asked, anger in my voice.

"That I don't know; I do know that Kardian isn't the only land home to those of dragon and shifter blood."

I felt a cold chill go through my body at these words. I knew what he meant; he was talking about the home of the Northern Gods and Goddesses, the land of ice and snow. The place of nature magic and the blood of mountains, men with powers of the earth and their brides of nature, those who could speak to the creatures around them.

Part of me shouldn't be worried; my birth father belonged to that land. Yet, here in the lands of the Three Goddesses was where I was born and grew up. I had heard the tales of warriors and wise ones, the love of family, and the loyalty of clans. Yet it was a wild land where many could lose life and limb.

"Astrid." Blaggdon's voice filled my ears, bringing back my worries.

"I'm sorry."

"You are right to be worried, but I would have my family and people take the lands of the forebears of shifters and dragons, then face the steel and fire of war."

"You don't have to face it alone…"

"I will not; if I know Flickron, he won't let anything happen to cause his mate pain."

"The Lady of Lace won't let her mate's heart get hurt either." I mused, and a weak smile appeared on my face.

Whittney Corum

"Let's get back to our fledglings," he replied, touching my shoulder and leading us to the young pups that were ours. Unaware of the flames that threatened everything that they had known.

Chapter 5
Emyr

I blinked, my mind processing what the Lady of Lace had just said. William gently touched my shoulder, bringing me out of my stupor.

"Why do come to me, Lady of Lace? I'm not one of your elves or the shifters blessed by your husband."

The Lady of Lace gently smiled at my words. Seeing that smile caused a calmness to fill my body. Then her voice filled the air like a melody lost to time, eerie but soothing to the ear.

"Your question is partly why I chose you. Most of Solara's believers would call my husband's shifters a curse. Yet you say it's a gift; your heart is filled with kindness and love, not just for those born from Solara's power but also for mine and Finas. You even took a stand for the dragons. That's why I'm asking to help them."

"But I'm a Novice of your sister's voice….I'm to be the next."

"I know, believe me, I wouldn't ask you to help if I hadn't weighed all my options. I know that if you decide to help me, you will be labeled a traitor; some might even call you a heretic."

The goddess started to walk, and I followed her, our steps hidden by the aura of the Lady of Lace. Williow was behind us, his steps seeming to echo the lady's. As we walked, it felt like I was walking with my late father; each step was a thought, and each breath a word of wisdom.

"That is what I will be; I'm a servant to Solara, your sister. Not to you. I've been raised to be her voice when the time came."

"I know. Yet I also know my sister. She might not like my creations or my husband, but she's not bloodthirsty."

"But the story of the first half-elf."

"The story often leaves out that the wolves were pets of our younger sister Faia. It also leaves out that the men who killed the parents were cursed never to see the sun again."

"You're talking about the vampires…"

"Don't speak their name out loud. Even gods don't call their name, even though they are bound to their home in the lost embers of Ash, they can still find a way to return."

"You mean that this war will bring them."

"Yes, which is why I want to make sure that we can save as many lives as we can."

"We?"

"I'm not the only god or Goddess who wants to protect our people. You have the blood of the king in your veins. You also have the blood of Anna, the first Northern blood to marry into the king of Zodiac's line. You possess both the Zodiac blessing of the Sun and the grace of the Sky Father."

I nodded, knowing that out of all the children before me, I was the one that took the most after the 2nd queen of

Zodiac. The woman didn't have shifter blood but was from the wilds of the North. One that was blessed not just by the Northern Gods but also by the Goddess Faia when she married the king of the Zodiac.

"You're not the first to say that about the blood."

"I know Solara's voice also talked to you about it."

"He said it might challenge me to be a voice with her blood in my veins. Yet when he said it, he didn't seem to mind, unlike the other high priests."

"Ango is a gentle soul; he also grew up in a village near the Ursa lands. I believe one of his adoptive uncles is a son of a lesser clan."

"That explains a lot."

"You mean his love of fish."

"And winter naps," I replied with a smile.

"Yes, Solara has often complained that her voice has a growl that makes him hard to understand. I remind her that she did take a Lion as a companion."

"A lion?" I asked, raising my brow."

"That's a story not meant for your ears, but I'll return to my question. Will you help save the land of Kardian?"

"Milady…I don't know."

The Lady of Lace sighed as the room sparked around us. She then looked at me with a mix of understanding and annoyance.

"It seems my sister's patience has run thin. I must leave. If you find your answer, go to Mer. There, you will find help. Lord Gael and his friends will lead you to where you need to be."

"And where…"

"Where all rulers meet. The hallow."

Chapter 6
Blaggdon

I watched as my mate lay in bed, fur covering her body as the moon gently covered her skin, adding a glow to her winter blond hair. I sighed, stopping the urge to run my fingers through it because it might break the sleep spell. Though the spell seemed to call to my wife, it was blocked by my curse of worry.

"Why must it come in my time? Why, when I have everything, I must lose it?" I asked mostly to myself.

I closed his eyes; thoughts and memories, both my and another, filled me. The spell that saved my life a year before had cost my dear cousin's life; we combined our lives and spirits together to save all dragons and protect the woman who had saved their heart. Yet when I explained it to Astrid, I left something out.

In using this forbidden spell, they had combined our lifelines together. It also took time off both lives, causing pain for the body that was used. I had been hiding his pain since it got worse. I knew my time was short, but I had thought it through; I didn't want to see my mate cry for me. She had done that enough when she felt her first love was killed.

"Now it seems war will drive your love away. If I could, I would stay here, in your embrace. In love you give and loyalty you show." I gently touched her face, calling on magic.

"Yet it seems that I'm to leave you my Flera. Yet, knowing this, I will always love you. My only hope is that you will find another when I take my last breath to be with you and guide our fledglings to a new age."

"But for now, I will stay with you. My heart beat to yours." I then let go, letting the magic fill my sleeping mate.

I then laid back down; the spell would protect my mate and guide her if something should happen. It would lead her to someone who would love and protect her as I would. I lay down, my body now tired of the magic I had used. I spared one more look at my mate before falling asleep, pulling her into my arms.

Chapter 7
Astrid

I sighed as I was in a forest I knew well. The simple colors of white and black fill the green and brown trees. I was counting to three when I felt a person behind me.

"So? What's the plan?" I asked, turning to Flickron's golden eyes.

"Well, that's one way to greet your sire daughter," Flickron replied with a hint of annoyance.

"Well, forgive me. My mind is on other things, like keeping my people and family safe.." I replied, my annoyance matching his.

He sighed, and as he did, the forest around us shook a little from his breath. His eyes closed for a moment before opening again. Flick then motioned for me to sit, and he followed suit, taking a seat as well.

"This is going to be a war even to rival the war between the Northern Gods and the three Goddesses."

I gripped my breeches and bit my lip. The war between the said two almost destroyed the land of Kardian. It only stopped when Flickron and the Lady of Lace married. It contained the bloodshed and brought the world we had known for hundreds of years.

"And there isn't a way to stop it?"

"Your mother has asked for help; if the one she asks agrees, there might be less bloodshed, but if not, I'm afraid we will lose many."

"Blaggdon wants us to leave to the Northern Wild."

"I agree with him. It will be hard, but you will be protected, and your people will be protected."

"I know that dragons and shifters trace back to the North, but what about Elves?"

"They are mine as much as your mother's. We are mates, and what she has, mine and I have, is hers. We agreed to this when we shared our blood." he said, his voice echoing in the dream, and his eyes flickered with pride and protectiveness in thinking about his wife and my birth mother.

"I understand…but what about those there? Will they allow us…"

"They know of all the creatures that are under my care and the love I have for your mother. They wouldn't

dare hurt you all. They will welcome you and, if needed, will help in the battle."

"It brings a little comfort.." I said, hugging myself.

"I thought when I followed my fate that I stopped a war."

"And you did, but sometimes even fate hides what happens from the gods."

"Really?"

"I think it's because she loves to see us stumble over ourselves. She really hates me, though."

"Really? Another woman who hates you."

"Your aunt Solora hates me because I took your mother. Fate hates me because of a few tricks I have and gave to my creations."

"You mean tricking death?" I asked, eyes narrowing.

"Sometimes, another time, I was trying to keep you with me and your mother. I also helped a few down on their luck change their fate," he said with a proud smile.

"Yeah.." I replied with a sigh.

"Anyway. I'm here to help." he then touched my forehead.

"I give you the way to the North. You will lead the dragons to their new home."

"What about Elves and Shifters?"

"They will have their own ways of finding the way. My worry is for you and the dragons. Some might not want to take a chance in Northern Wilds. Others will want to keep their families safe, so they will obey, and others will be wary."

"Because of what happened with the dragon hunters."

"Fear for a family member will make anyone do something that might cause pain to others."

"I know."

"Good, be careful, daughter. I'm afraid that this time, it's not just your fate or life on the line. It's the dragons' lives themselves."

"I know, but you forget, Flick, I have already saved one. I just need to do it about a thousand more times." I said with a smirk that matched his own.

Chapter 8
Emyr

    I walked down the halls of the Novice house as the moonlight shone down. It was called the Novice House because it housed all the students for both the priests and priestesses. I had walked this hallway many times before, but instead of bringing me solace and understanding, I found myself lost in thoughts. They race through my mind like the swirling waves of a storm at sea.

    "Solara, why would the Lady of Lace ask me to save them? To help those who aren't your creation.."

    "Because your heart is full of kindness, milord," Willow added to my thoughts, a slight smile on his face.

"It would seem so, though I don't think my brother will like it."

"Nor his witch," William said with a taste of disgust.

"William, still remember, even in the halls of learning, there are ears who still cling to the words of the palace," I replied, my eyes looking for those novices who were still awake.

"Sorry, milord."

"It's alright; I'm going to speak to Master."

"The Voice of Solara? So you are thinking of the Lady of Lace's request?" Willow asked, his body shifting from one foot to the other in excitement.

"Yes, I think Master might have more insight than I have."

"He's old enough for it."

"Willow," I warned, giving my friend a glare for him to behave.

"You know I'm just stating the facts."

"Some facts shouldn't be spoken, elf." a voice replied, and we both looked forward to seeing the Voice of Solara.

Argos, the Voice of Solara, was a man in his late 50s with locks of auburn hair and sunkissed skin. His deep blue eyes held a mixture of playfulness but also the wisdom that came from being the voice of the Goddess. He wore the robes of the voice, golds, and reds, which stood out against his skin.

"Master," I said, bowing, pulling Willow with me.

"Rise, both of you," Argos replied with a tired smile.

"So what is it that has both of you awake?"

I took a breath and told my master what happened. His brow creased while his smile turned into a thoughtful frown. His eyes were winded with knowledge as he processed my words.

"War, I thought the prince's hatred wasn't that deep, but I have forgotten who has his ear."

"What should I do?" I asked.

"I think you need to go on a pilgrimage."

"A pilgrimage?"

"Yes, to the Temple of Mer. The head Priestess there had asked for a Novice to help out. It will be good for your training."

"Master…" I started.

"The Lady of Lace has asked you to help all Kardian. She even risked her sister's wrath. I believe you should follow it."

"But what about Solara…"

"Our lady might not like the others, but I wouldn't think she would want to cause her sister pain."

"But we're taught not…." I started before he put his hand up to stop me.

"Not to put our own understanding in what Solara speaks to us about. I'm not, at least not to a group of followers. I'm speaking to my heir, who will have my title one day."

"But…"

"Just go to Mer, meet with the lord. If only to get you out of the palace and capital."

"Master?"

"You might be my heir, but only a fool would think that you would be safe with that. You are the king's son first."

I then realized what he meant. True, I was promised to Solara when I was born. I was to be the new voice of Solara, but what Argos said was right—I was also the king's son. An heir to the crown and child blessed by Solara. If the court wanted, they could ask for me to be king. Others might want me dead just because of those who want me as king.

"I guess I don't have a choice," I said, my voice a whisper.

"You do, but this isn't one. You need to leave now when the moon is out. I believe the Lady Lace will aid you in this."

I nodded, leaving my master. Willow was beside me as he walked the halls, which were even quieter. Almost as if it was the silence of death on our heels.

Chapter 9
Blaggdon

The council was made of those who came from the first dragons, friends to my ancestors, and over the years, they became part of the Dragen's family. Yet, as we sit in the cave of our forefathers, I can only feel the fear and mistrust.

Fear of what I had just told them about the warnings both from the God of Death and Flickron. The fear of leaving the lands we call our own to go to another place we only heard of. Mistrust because of blood that was shed a few months ago.

My Flera's sister, Ingrid, had called on dragon hunters to save her sister. It had turned out that she, along with the rest of her company, was tricked by one of my mate's trusted friends and caused the death of one of the council.

Even though most of the council understood we all had been tricked, some were still worried about trusting my mate. Out of the 4 members of the council, the only two who were my allies were Roka, the eastern dragon of the sea who helped my Flera when she was carrying my twins. The other was Kaya, one of the youngest of the council and an earth dragon from the West.

Electra, the fire dragon of the south, trusted me but also had a voice that my flarea might need to be watched. Not because she would betray us but because of what had happened before when she trusted someone. She wasn't the only one who agreed with it.

The other who voiced that my Flera needed someone to protect her other than myself was Nels. The ice dragon of the North and my Flera's cousin by way of her adoptive mother. He had gotten his position after his father's death a few months ago. The winter blond still hated me for it, but it didn't stop him from doing his duties.

"So, we have to face a war with humans," Nels stated, frowning, causing him to look older than his 23 years.

"Yes, though we can't stop, we can ensure some of us survive."

"You mean leaving our homes to go to the Northern lands!" Nels stood up, his hands scratching the table.

"It's the only way to protect our Flares, Flareas, and fledglings," I replied, giving him a glare.

"It might, but it still feels like we're running."

"Not all of us," I replied.

"You want to stay and flight," Roka spoke, his hands touching his beard.

"Yes, I have decided to fight alongside those who would fight to protect those who can head to the Northern land."

"But you're the Dragen?! If you stay, what will the rest do?" Elktra growled.

"They will live, you forget my hier and children will be. Until my heir is of age, my Flarea will rule.."

"Alone? You know some of the dragons still don't trust her." Kaya said, rubbing her hands together in worry.

"Not alone; I plan to invoke the law of bonds," I said, bracing myself.

"Are you mad? Your wife is of shifter blood; you're basically telling her that your mating means nothing." Nels growl.

"There is a reason we stopped the practice during my father's time. It causes more harm than good." Roka spoke.

"The simple fact is that it was created for the Flares and Flareas of the Dragen. If the Dragen was killed, the flare or Flera were given to his next relative or closest friend. But during the time of the 5th Dragen, he abused this law to take his brother's mate and forced them to be the queen." Roka said, his eyes narrowing at each word.

"The shifter died soon after; in their beliefs, mates are forever and being away from them is a death sentence. So you want to bring it back to use on your wife?" Nels growled.

"Unless you have another idea, I want my Flarea safe, but I can't say with her. Like some have said, they won't trust her alone…"

"She won't be alone," Elktra said, standing up.

"What do you mean?"

"Kaya and Nels will be with her."

"What?!" the two named asked.

"You two are the youngest of the council and the right age to help guide our queen. Roka and I will stay with our king."

"But…" Kaya was shaking.

"Little sister, it's the job of the young to live and give new life. Those who are old and can't give to this generation will be needed to protect those who can." Elktra comforted the younger woman.

"What about the wisdom that elders can give us?" I asked, looking at Roka.

"My knowledge has already been passed down; it is to my grandchildren who will help the next generation."

"Elktra?" I turned to the woman, who gave me a look filled with understanding but also stubborn.

"I have made my peace; many of blood can become a council member if I'm gone."

"What about your Flare?"

"I will talk to him."

"Nels? What say the voice of the North."

"We both know I've lost the fight on this. But I will protect my cousin," he replied with a huff.

"Good," I replied, nodding at the council.

"I now dismiss this meeting of the Council. I will give you all until the full moon before we start on the path of war."

"Yes, my king." the four of them chorus.

Whittney Corum

I watched them transform and fly from our chamber. I winced, feeling a pain in my body, but I took a breath. I had made it through the council, but now it was time for the real challenge, my Flera.

Chapter 10
Astrid

"Mama, what's wrong?" the voice of my eldest pup asked.

I looked up from the map I was reading and looked up at the emerald green eyes of the pup. I sighed and gently patted his hair, golden locks curling to my fingers. He giggled, a smile spreading across his face.

"Mama is just looking at a map," I explained.

"Why?"

I bit my lip; part of me wanted to keep my pups from finding out the dangers that were coming for us. Yet another part of me knew that I couldn't keep the shadows away, but I would make sure they were prepared for it.

"We're going on a trip."

"Where?"

"We're going to the Northern Wilds."

"Across the sea?"

"Yes, we're going with some others on this trip."

"What about papa?"

"I must stay here a few days but will find you all."

"Papa!" our pup said, running over to him.

"Hello, Aidan, are you being good for your mother?"

"Yes, I even helped put Amond and Alsing to nest," Aiden replied, puffing his chest out and smiling at his father.

"Good boy, now why don't you go to your room? I'll see you later."

"But I want to stay up with you and Mama," the pup pouted.

"Aidan, mama, and Papa need to talk about parent stuff."

"Oh, like when you talked about the twins?"

I felt heat go to my cheeks and saw the same red on my mate's face too. We both looked at each other, pleading the other to speak first. The battle was won by me however when my mate sighed.

"Somewhat, now go to sleep."

"Alright." the pup replied before approaching me and kissing my cheek.

"Night, Adien," I said, kissing his head.

"Night mama, and papa. Also, I want another brother this time."

I glared at my mate when the boy was out of the room. Blaggdon raised his hands in surrender, a nervous smile on his face.

"I don't know where he got the idea from."

"Of course you don't," I replied, narrowing my eyes.

"Astrid, there are other things we need to discuss other than our son's desire for a younger sibling."

"The war," I replied as he nodded, his jaw tightening.

"I have talked with the council, and it's been decided that Kaya and Nels will go with those who will go to the Northern Wilds."

"What about Roka and Elctra?"

"They will stay and fight, along with myself."

I gripped the fabric of my breeches, almost tearing them. I closed my eyes, willing my anger to subside. I knew that Blaggdon would choose to stay; he is the ruler of Dragons and would need to lead the army. Yet another part of me wanted to scream at him that he should stay with his pups and myself.

"Astrid?"

"I understand…"

"That doesn't make it right," Blaggdon replied, touching my hand hands.

"No, it doesn't," I said, my voice echoing with pain.

"Astrid…"

"You know, I had a conservation like this before. That time, my love pushed me away like now."

"Astrid, this isn't that; it's to protect you and the fledglings…"

"Don't you think I don't know that!" I stood up, my voice filled with fire and pain.

"I know the importance a king is to their kingdom. I know how important a queen is to his aid and kingdom. I know as a mate that sometimes my mate would need to leave to protect their homes and family. That doesn't mean that my heart doesn't break. It doesn't mean the times I'm told to leave my mate for protection don't break my heart. I'm not just a queen and daughter of Flickron and Lady of Lace, the adoptive daughter of the Finnis heir and the elfin princess. I'm your mate, your second half, so forgive me if I hate the idea of leaving you again."

I felt tears in my eyes, a mixture of the pain and rage that fought in my heart. Blaggdon sat on his chair, looking up at me. His eyes fight the emotions of his own anger and sadness.

Blaggdon started to open his mouth, but I stopped him.

"Don't…I need to ensure that everything will be ready for our trip." I then turned, leaving my mate.

Chapter 11
Emyr

Willow and I found ourselves outside Lord Gael's home. We were brought here when the head priestess of the temple saw us. I didn't know why until I saw the Flame Knights, the order under my brother. They were also known by another name, the sword of the king. This meant that they were killers for the king.

Willow then grabbed my hand and led me away. I was still reeling from knowing that my brother had called the knights to end me. Then my second thought was of Argos: had he been killed? Or was there a spy in the temple?

"Do you think Argos…"

"Being the old man, he'll take more than a few knights," Willow said as he stepped into the courtyard.

As his foot stepped into the dirt, we both heard a growl. Our eyes landed on a gray wolf that stood before us, its fur littered with scars. I quickly put Williow behind me as if my slightly taller height would protect him.

"Freki, it's alright." a voice filled the air.

My eyes went from the wolf to an elf with golden hair. She was dressed in a sleeping gown with a robe over it. Behind her was an older man dressed in his own nightclothes.

"Your Highness?" the man said as the wolf walked over to him.

"Lord Gael.." I said with a tired smile.

"Come inside; the ears of Mer are sometimes quicker than their eyes." He motioned me inside. As we did, I felt a magical barrier activate.

Once we were inside the warmth of home, the wolf transformed into a man, his eyes staring at Willow and me. The elf girl was by the fire, getting a kettle from it. My eyes didn't leave her; it was as if something was calling to me to the beauty before me.

"So what is the prince of all Kardian come to me?" Lord Gael asked as he took the kettle from the elf.

I took a breath and told all three about what the Lady of Lace told me. At each word, the shifter went closer to the elf as a father would protect a child. I understood why I was telling them their lives were forfeit.

"What will you do?" Lord Gael asked, his eyes narrowing.

"I don't know…I have been trained to be the voice of Solara all my life. But now, it seems I have to go against it." I replied, gripping my cup.

"Because you want to protect others. Solara has talked about protecting others." Lord Gael.

"Humans, those of our own blood, she doesn't care about the other creatures," I replied.

"Yet the voice of Solara has talked about us living in peace."

"I know, and I believe that as well," I replied, looking down at my cup.

"You know, out of the two of you, I believe you take after the king more than your brother," Lord Gael said, a gentle smile on his face.

"Argos told me that I could be king."

"But you don't want to."

"I'm the second son, who was raised as a priest."

"Yet you're asked to save the whole land and its people."

"I know, but if I do, I will be labeled as a traitor to the crown and a heretic to the priests and priestess of Solara. To save everyone, I have to betray all that I love."

"You will find, my lord, that sometimes what you have come to know isn't something you should keep."

"Have you faced this before, Lord Gael?" I asked, looking into the older man's eyes.

"A few months ago, I lost a friend while hunting a dragon. It wasn't the dragon who killed him, but a servant to a goddess who sought to gain power. I learned that sometimes monsters aren't the ones that look different from us. Sometimes, the monsters are humans who choose to serve selfishness and their own greed."

"So you believe that the monster in this case is the hate my brother and his wife have. They are the ones who will destroy, but the innocents are the shifters, elves, and dragons."

"That is what I believe. It's up to you to make up your mind."

"You know you're the third person who has told me it's my decision."

"Then I'm in good company. Now, let's all retire for the night. We have a long journey." Lord Gael declared, rising to his feet and standing beside the other man and Ingrid.

"A journey?" Willow asked, standing up.

"We're heading to Rinbow, the city of Elves. I need to warn my grandfather what's going on." Ingrid replied.

"Grandfather…wait, you can't be Princess Ingrid?!" Williow said, his eyes widening.

"Princess?" I asked, looking at him.

"She's a child of one the high king's granddaughters, the child of the 4th princess and the head of the Finis clan."

My own eyes widened; I heard that the elves lived long lives. I had also heard that elves had strong ties to shifters. Yet standing before me was a child of their royalty and, by all rights, a royal of a shifter clan.

"How..."

"It's a longer story that we have no time to tell, at least not tonight," Gael replied and gave them a good night.

"Sir."

"We better go to bed too, Willow. We will need to get up early. We have a long journey ahead."

Chapter 12
Blaggdon

I sighed, my thoughts going to my mate. She was right; she had given so much and was being pushed away again. I hated seeing her feel powerless, feeling like she needed to face everything on her own.

"What a mate I am..." I sighed.

"Yes, what a mate are you." I heard a growl and turned to see the golden eyes of Flickron.

"Flickron…"

"My daughter was crying, and you let her leave that way."

"Do you think I wanted that? I love her and would give anything to stay with her." I shouted at him, my fists shaking with anger.

"Then why would you choose to leave her again?"

"Because I have to. I'm the Dragen; it's my duty to protect my people and family. Even if it costs my life. She knows that…"

"Just because she knows doesn't mean that it doesn't break her heart."

"I know, but I can't forget my duty."

"I know about duty and how much pain it can cause in leaving those you love for the greater good. It might be right, and it might help, but it doesn't stop the fact it still causes pain." Flickron said, his eyes flashing with hurt and understanding.

"You're talking about the first dragen's mate."

"Partly, I'm also talking about my wife and daughter. Luna loves me, but that doesn't mean she was hurt when she had to leave her sisters. My daughter is hurt because she almost lost you once, and now she is going to lose you again."

"I can't stop it. At least this way, she won't see it." I replied, looking away, feeling a slight ache go through my body.

"You're talking about the spirit curse. The price of combing yourself with Keyne."

"We both knew the risks, but I didn't think it would be this fast. At least if she is away, she won't see me die like this."

"So you would rather die in war than in the arms of your mate?"

"Do you want to see your daughter in more pain?"

Flickron sighed and ran his fingers through his hair. His eyes closed as he took a deep breath.

"No, but either way, her heart will break."

"I know, and if I could, I would stop it."

Flickron didn't say anything, his body relaxing as he took deep breaths.

"Your forefathers wanted to be punished because of another's sin. Yet you all rose above that to become better. I can't give you any more gifts; I can't stop your death. I can promise you this, though. I will do everything to ensure the dragons thrive in the North."

"Good, at least my people will be safe," I replied with a sigh, my body feeling heavy with guilt about leaving my family and knowing my people would thrive.

"I understand my father more now; sometimes being in a seat of power isn't something to take likely."

"Yes."

"I will leave you, Dragen. May your flame burn bright as a star."

I watch the god of Trickers leave my sight. Part of me knew that he was up to something, yet I also knew he couldn't meddle as much in death as in other things. My thoughts then turned to my mate. I would have to face her again. However, I didn't know if I would be greeted as love or as cause of her pain.

Chapter 13
Astrid

I walked between the loaded carts of supplies, Asling and Almond, in a sling across my body. Almond was in front to see what he would do, while Asling was on my back, snuggling into it. They both could hear my heartbeat and kept snuggling me in their sleep.

I checked to ensure everything was ready for the journey to the Bone Cliffs. Once there, we would take a path known to some of the Flare and Flarea to the beach, where boats would be ready. Yet, it also caused me to wonder what type of ship would be allowed to enter the shores of the Merfolk.

"Milady?" a voice called me from my thoughts.

Lunar series book 3: King's Folly

I looked behind me to see Calum, Elktra's Flare. Calum was only a few years older than me, with dusty brown hair and a mixture of gold and gray eyes. Calum was a mixture of shifter, elf, and human. His mother was a human, while his father was a shifter mix of elf and the flying clan of Tario.

"Calum, how are we doing?"

"Everyone should be ready in four days."

I nodded before I looked at small, sleeping in my arms.

"How many fledglings will be with us?"

"50, though 5 Flareas are with child, and a few dragons are with child."

I nodded, noting that we needed to ensure that healers were close to the young and those close to giving birth. Calum, reading my mind, quickly added.

"I already have some of the healers to be within earshot of most of the Flareas, and one of the daughters of Roka will be in charge of the dragons."

"That's good. Do you know how many will be with us?"

"In total, there will be 30 dragons."

"30…"

"Some want to stay here. They believe that they would be safer here."

"In other words, they don't trust me," I replied, biting my lip.

"Would you like me to lie and say they don't?"

"No, I understand, but that shouldn't stop them from going."

"It's not just that milady. Some believe they won't be able to make it. Others believe that the younger generation should be the ones going."

"And where do you stand?" I asked, stopping to look into his eyes.

"I don't blame you for the choices others make. You are the mate of the Dragen, mother to his heirs, and helped the dragons from a false king."

"I'm also the sister to the elf who brought dragon hunters to our home and also the one who appointed a traitor to be my messenger."

"It was out of love that your sister came to save you. Also, the lion chose his own bed to follow a dark Goddess. They both were rewarded and punished in their own ways."

"Yes, they were," I replied, my thoughts going to my sister and her company.

"Have you heard from your sister?"

"A few months ago, she, along with her party, were back at Mer. She was talking about visiting our mother's family."

"She might want to get there faster," Calum said with a worried frown.

"I know, but she's with a Maccon, and Lord Gael has power in human lands."

"But you're still worried."

"Yes, and not just her. My brothers and uncle were heading to the pack lands. I know the clan will protect them…"

"You think that the council won't move fast enough."

"It's not that; they usually are quick to understand the situation; what I'm worried about is the time in between."

"You mean how long it would take to get everyone in one place."

"All shifters are scattered into their different territories, and some are closer to Zodiac than others. What if they can't get to safety in time?" I asked, holding my babies closer.

"You forget, the shifters are creations of Flickron. We are known to be able to find ways out of trouble."

"And also cause it," I replied with a smile.

"Maybe." He smiled and then looked ahead.

"We have caused a lot..but we didn't cause this war."

"No, the only ones to blame are the human king's greed and hate for all of us." We both turned to see my mate along with Electra.

"My Dragen," Calum said, bowing.

"Hello, Calum. I see my Flarea and you have been doing a good job."

"It's mostly Calum; I'm just checking his work," I replied, looking at Electra.

"Don't sell yourself short, my queen. I know my mate has a mind for numbers and charts. I also know you help as much as you can. Though you have another job that is equally important." The fire dragon replied, gently touching Almond's head.

"Thank you," I replied.

"Don't thank me, milady; I'm only stating facts. Though I need to take my mate away for a few moments."

"Of course," I said.

Calum nodded his thanks and went away from us with his love. My heart ached for them; like me, Calum would be leaving while his mate would stay and fight.

Though some flare and Flareas wanted to stay and fight, some had to leave to help with others. Calum would go because he knew about the Northern wild.

He had been there a few years when he was a child. He and his father had gone to trade with a distant cousin and stayed for about 2 years. So he knew the land well and would be able to help us land safely and talk with the locals. Yet it also took him away from his mate.

"Astrid, may I walk with you?" Blaggdon asked.

I looked up at him, his eyes pleading for my answer. I took a breath and gently kissed both of my pups' heads. I could still feel the asking eyes on me.

"Until the end of time," I said as we walked.

Chapter 14
Emyr

"Williow, will you sit," I told my friend, who had been jumping up in our wagon.

"Sit! Milord, we're on our way to the home of elves!" Willow shouted in the air, a smile splitting his face.

"Oi, you are too loud for an elf," a growl answered.

"Freki, leave the boy alone." Lord Gael sighed.

"Boy? He's old enough to know better."

I sighed, looking at Felki, the son of the Maccon clan. A rough-looking man covered in scars reminded me of the wolf that met us at Lord Gael's home. The older wolf seemed to have no problem with Ingird or his lord, but the two of us seemed to bring his ire.

"Willow," I said again, pulling his sleeve.

Willow sat down, a smile still on his face. I knew why he was excited; he was a half-elf but hadn't seen his mother's home. This wasn't for lack of trying, but a mixed-blood child alone in the world wouldn't be able to get the home of elves, especially at 6 years old.

"Willow, you can visit your mother's family when we arrive."

"And leave you alone in the halls of the king? I have been by your side since we first met. I won't leave you now. Besides, I don't even know who my mother's family is."

"You're mother didn't.."

"My mother was disowned because she married a human," he replied, his smile becoming smaller.

"What! I knew some humans didn't like elves marrying their blood, but I didn't think elves…"

"Some elves are like humans; they don't want their blood mixed," Felki remarked.

"Mama said that even some of her cousins hated that our Lady of Lace would marry a fool and then ask her people to do the same thing," Ingrid added.

"Thankfully, not everyone has those beliefs," I replied.

"Are you sure you're supposed to be the voice of Solara?" Felki asked, raising an eyebrow.

"I'm still a novice…"

"Keep talking about that, and the temple might kick you out."

I bit my lip, and the feeling of unease at the shifter's words filled me. My mind went to my conservations with the Lady of Lace and my master. Their words swirl in both my mind and heart. I then felt a hand on my shoulder and looked over at Willow.

"Thank you," I whispered.

"Milord, you are kind. It doesn't matter what everyone else thinks; you are kind and just. A king in thoughts and ideas."

"You read some of the scrolls, didn't you," I said with a knowing smile.

"What else would I do when you and the old man were talking?" he smirked.

"Quiet," Gael ordered as he stopped his horse.

"Lord?" Felki said, standing closer to the man.

"It seems we have some friends," he said, narrowing his eyes.

A figure then appeared, dressed in the clothes of the knight. His eyes traced all of us before smirking when he saw me.

"Hello, my prince, I'm glad you are here. It makes my job easier."

"And what's that?" I asked.

"Way to make sure my king doesn't have threats to the throne. So it's time to die."

Chapter 15
Blaggdon

I woke up to my body screaming in pain. My hands reach to my chest as I try to find my breath. My eyes shut, willing the pain to leave.

"My mate.." the voice of my mate asked, laced with both tiredness and worry.

"I'm fine," I whispered, hoping my voice hid my pain.

I could feel her shift and then felt her hand reach out to me. I quickly took it, afraid she would feel the pain that ravaged my body.

"What's wrong?" she asked, still hovering between wakefulness and sleep.

"Nothing, just a bad dream. I'm going to take a little walk."

"I will go with you." She started to get up.

"No, you need your sleep," I said, gripping her hand.

"What about you…"

"I'm fine, my Flarea, now sleep," I replied, kissing her hand.

"Blaggdon…"

"Sleep my dear, sleep my heart, though we may part. The winter wind sings its song, bringing death and sadness. Yet, do not fall into sadness because you are in my heart. The beauty of my eye, the blessed daughter of a mother, perfect in all things, my children's mother."

I gently ran my hand through her hair. Watching as the star-colored eyes closed, sleep called her. Soon, her breath evened out, and she fell back asleep.

I then got up, the pain coming back. I made it out of our shared room before I fell to the floor of the hallway.

"Gods, why now? At least not while they are here." I growled.

"I know this is my price, but please don't let them be here."

I pleaded to stones around me as if they would be able to answer. Pain filled me again as the feeling of needles went through every fiber of my body. The needles were then replaced with a deep burying. I bit my lip, breaking the skin.

"My dragen?" a voice came through the fog of pain.

I then felt aged hands touch my brow as cool filled my body. I looked up to see Roka, a frown on his face. I closed my eyes and sighed.

"It's my price.."

"How long have you had the pain?"

"It started getting worse after the twins were born.." I breathed.

"My Dragen, we must get you to my healer's room. I have something that will help you ease the pain."

I nodded, my throat now burning from the words I had spoken before. Roka, using strength that would make a man in his prime envious, helped me up. We then took the path to the healer's room; with each step, white-hot pain filled me.

Soon, we were in the healer's room, the domain of Roka. It was a room made of stone walls, which were hallowed out to hold all the potions and salves that Roka and his family created. In the center was a slab of stone, which was big enough to hold a full-grown dragon in their human form.

Roka laid me on the slab; its cool surface helped with the heat. My eyes slowed, following the skilled hands that reached for bottles that held healing herbs that I couldn't name. Soon, the smell of spices and herbs filled the air.

"It won't stop your bruises, but it will ease your pain," Roka said. The sound of clay blows filled my ears.

I then felt cool hands, which helped me sit up and the smell of spices filled my nose.

"Drink all of it, my Dragen." Roka ordered, a worried frown on his face.

I obeyed, the warm liquid filling my body. Soon, the white-hot pain that raged through my body was now fading to a dull ache. A breath of relief filled me as I was able to breathe easily. I looked over at the elder and gave him a thankful smile.

"Roka.."

"Dragen, I did what I did because I'm a healer. My family has served yours since the first Dragen. Though I have to say you're one of the foolish ones."

"Because I used a forbidden spell to merge two souls into one to protect my Flera? I would do it again; I know the cost of it." I replied.

"That's not why you're foolish; you haven't told your queen. You know this will break her heart."

"I have already had this talk with Flickron."

"Of course you have. Flickron is very fond of the blood which flows through your Flera's veins."

"Yes," I said quickly.

The only ones who knew of my wife's true parentage were only the two of us. We had decided to keep it between us because some of the dragon's Flare and Flareas thought of the Northern God only as the fool who married their Goddess. Others thought that the two loved one another.

Astrid didn't want to cause a rift between our people, so she asked me to keep it a secret. I agreed, and everyone thought that she was the daughter of Finnis and the blood of elves.

"That being said, you need to tell her."

"I will not have her thoughts on my pain," I replied, gripping the slab.

"No, but you will have her thoughts on your death."

"What do you mean?"

"You are staying to fight; your Flarea will be leaving with your fledglings. Her thoughts will be you on the battlefield in the eyes of those who wouldn't think twice to kill you."

"It's better than her thinking it's her fault." I bit back.

"My dragen." Roka said with an understanding tone.

"I'd rather her think I died protecting my people than die because of choosing to stay to love her."

"Very well. I will not say anything more about it."

"Thank you, now I must get back to Flera, and I believe you as well."

"Yes, though some of our grandchildren have taken to sleeping between us."

"For warmth or protection?" I asked.

"I wish it was first; that way, it would be easier to tease them."

"I promise they will be safe."

"I know you might be a fool, but you are still the Dragen," he replied, leaving me alone.

I sighed, my own thoughts going to my Flarea. I walked the path to our room, my footsteps light on the stone. Soon, I was by my mate's side, her warmth filling me with calm as I pulled her close.

Chapter 16
Astrid

It was time; everyone was ready to leave the place we called home. My heart ached watching couples and families break apart. Even though it was to protect the next generation, it didn't change the fact families were losing a part of them.

"Mamma?" I looked down at Aiden, who held my hand.

"Yes, what's the matter, little one."

"Everyone is sad. Why? We're only going on a trip."

I bit my lip, my mind searching for the words to tell my pup. When a voice came behind us, it spoke for me.

"Because every time someone leaves, it is a little sad."

"Dad," Adien replied with a smile.

"Aiden, do you understand what I'm saying?" Blaggdon asked, kneeling to our son's height.

"That leaving someone is hard and sad?"

"Yes, I knew you were smart. But also remember, even if someone leaves, they will always be in one place." I watched as my mate touched our son's chest.

"My heart."

"Right, I will keep your four in my heart while you go on the trip."

"And I'll keep you in mine."

"Blaggdon…" I started but was cut off by Almond, who started to fuss.

I quickly turn my attention to the babe trashing around in his carrier. Asling was awake also, but unlike her brother, she was quiet watching him. I sighed; at times like these, I wondered if Asling had gotten some of my birth parents' blood more than her brother.

"What's the matter Almond?" I cooed to him, picking him up and gently rocking him.

He looked up at me, his eyes filled with unshead tears. I hummed, hoping the song would calm him and my own heart. Soon, the baby returned to sleep and I laid him beside Asling, who looked at me, sparkling as if she had caught something funny.

"What about you, little princess?" I asked, gently touching her head.

She reached out to touch my hand. I smiled, letting my hand touch hers, which I should have known better. Once her hand touched my fingers, a spark went off. I pulled away, wincing a little, a burn on my hand.

"Dammit," I said.

Asling, seeing my grimace, seemed to understand and started to cry. I quickly forgot about my hand and went to pick her up, only for Blaggdon to beat me to it. His voice filled the air, singing a song to our child. Soon, the quiet cries turned into a yawn, and the babe fell asleep.

"Let me look at your hand, my lady." I turned to Roku, who had snuck up on us.

I nodded, bringing my hand to his older one. I watched as he looked at the burn which took over most of my hand. I winced as he touched a tender part, biting my lips as I felt cold touch it.

"Easy, I'll be done soon."

"It's alright," I said with a forced smile.

Soon, the pain waned, and I looked down at my hand. There was a slight scar, but it wasn't bad. I had seen worse from both my adoptive father and uncle while hunting a wild boar, which caused a deep wound on my uncle's back, which took up his whole back. It was healed, but still glaring white against his slight tan skin.

"Astrid?" I turned to look at the worry-filled face of Blaggdon.

"I'm fine; it seems our daughter has been blessed with my blood," I said with a sigh.

"That's good; at least she's going to be strong."

"And witty, which I don't know if that's a good thing."

"What do you mean? Shouldn't we be proud of our daughter being smart?" he asked, raising his eyebrows.

"Blaggdon, I have to deal with one witty shifter in my family; my nerves can't hold anymore."

Blaggdon just smiled and kissed my head. His arms holding me tight as if it would be the last time he would see me. I looked up into his eyes, hoping to catch anything hidden, but I only found love and loss.

"Blaggdon."

"I love you so much, my Flera. You are the mother to my children, the queen to my people, and the love of my heart. Know that keep you and our children in my heart."

"I know that, and I feel the same. I will wait for you." I promised.

I then felt his grip tight and felt him shake. I didn't know why, but he was trying to hold something in. Yet when I looked into his eyes, I only saw love and sorrow.

"Blaggdon...."

"I will return to you."

I nodded, but part of me wondered when and how he would return.

Chapter 17
Emyr

It only took a moment, but as soon as the knight spoke, the night was filled with the sound of birds. At least that's what I thought, but I was proven wrong as Willow pushed me down. As we went down, an arrow narrowly missed my head.

"Ingrid, get down." Lord Gael stated as he got off his horse.

Ingrid followed as Frecki dogged the arrows. I had heard of shifters being sound on their feet, but this was the first time I had seen them in action. I then looked over at Willow, my eyes widening at seeing my friend lying beside me, blood pooling underneath him. I moved to help him, but another set of arrows was loosed.

Yet before they could hit us again, a barrier was set around us. A dark green with runes of earth and protection glowed in the night. Then, the sound of winds filled the air, twisting and attacking the knight and those around him.

It was as if wolves were howling at night and found their prey. My heart seemed to echo their cries as fear and anger poured out. I then felt the earth shake, and a voice filled our ears.

"Get to the trees. Follow the path."

I quickly grabbed Willow, mindful of the blood. My feet headed to the voice, and a figure beside me took some of Willow's weight. I didn't get a good look as we quickly went to the trees, which seemed to move to hide us from the knights.

"We can stop now," a voice in front of us said.

Those words went straight to my body, which fell to my knees. My thoughts went to Willow. As I turned, I saw he was in the arms of an elf I hadn't seen before. I tried to move, but my body kept me in place; even my voice seemed to be stuck.

"Uncle Furrow." Ingrid's voice filled the air, and I turned to her.

The elf was hugging a shifter with winter blond hair. The shifter was a little younger than my late father and was twice as tall as the elf he held. His smile was a mixture of relief and happiness.

"Ingrid, my little star. I'm glad you are safe."

"Furrow, as much as I like seeing my student safely in hand, we have other things to worry about."

"Willow.." I said, almost like a prayer.

"Ash?" the voice of the elder shifter asked.

"Willow, I have heard that name; he is of my blood. Ember's son."

"Can you help him?" I asked and was answered by sliver blue eyes staring through me.

"I will not leave my blood to die in the shadows of the forest."

"Ash, he's not only the prince of Zodiac; he's the one our lady has asked to help us," Furrow said, walking over to the elf.

"Maybe, though, it doesn't change the fact that his blood wants us dead."

"Yet he is worried about your blood."

The elf just huffed as their attention turned back to Willow. I thought I could hear a prayer coming from the elf. I then felt a hand on my shoulder; I looked up to see Furrow.

"Come, you have an important meeting to go to."

"What do you mean?"

"You are going to meet with our voices of Lady of Lace and Flickron. The king of Elves and the elders of shifters."

Chapter 18
Blaggdon

I walk through the rooms of my home, my ears getting used to the quiet. My Flarea, along with my fledglings, were gone, on their way to safety. I wasn't the only one feeling the quiet; my people had been divided from their families.

"It's to save our children…"

"At a cost some might call too much." I sighed, turning around to see Electra.

"You could have gone with your Flare.."

"As you could have gone with your Flarea and fledglings. You're the dragen; you could have ordered us to stay with them and lead our people…"

"You know I couldn't do that. I couldn't leave those who couldn't fight."

"Yet you still face the embrace of death."

"So do you," I replied.

"What can I say? I follow my Dragen's example." She replied with a smirk.

"Electra…"

"Don't; Roka and I made our choice to stay with you, knowing what price it might cost."

"I know, believe me, if I had another choice…"

"You wouldn't, not if your people and family would be put in danger," she replied matter-of-factly.

"You're right; I'd rather them be out of reach of bloodshed than risk them being here."

"Which is the reason for most of the dragons who stayed here. We want to make sure our families don't have to be in the sights of those who would not think twice about murdering us."

I could hear the anger and pain in her voice. Electra had experince being hunted when she was a fledgling. Her family had been too close to a human village and cited their anger. They had come in the night and taken the lives of Electra's parents and elder siblings. She was found a few days later by her aunt and was raised by her.

"I didn't mean to bring up painful memories."

"I know, but they still are in my heart. So what are we going to do?"

"Well, this arrived a few days ago." I handed a parchment to her.

The fire dragon read it, her face creasing at each word. Once she was finished, she looked up at me with a slight frown.

"Did you tell this to your mate?"

"I didn't want to worry her."

"This is a message from the King of Elves, her blood asking for audience."

"I know, and the shifter elders will be there also. They want to discuss what to do with this threat."

"And you didn't want your mate to know."

"She would try to stay; I couldn't let her do that."

"My Dragen."

"I know I'm thinking more as a mate than a king, but I'd rather have my mate and fledglings safe as they can be."

"I know, it might be partly because you are a father and mate, but you also act like a ruler. You chose to ensure your line is safe, and if anything happened to you, they could go on." She replied, a slight sadness in her voice.

"Electra…I shouldn't talk of…"

"Children, my king, both my Flare and I have realized that the gods have chosen us not to bring lives into the world, and then we would help the others who do."

I simply nodded; I had no words to answer or knowledge to help her. Then I heard a snicker.

"What?" I asked.

"I'm just imagining who will kill you first, your mate's grandfathers or mate."

"What do…oh." I stopped myself and felt a shiver.

The king of Elves and head of the Finnis clan are the blood relatives of parents who raised my mate. They might not be as powerful as her true parents and line, but I would be dead even before the war if they were anything like the trickster.

"Oh Goddess…" I said.

"This is going to be great," Electra said, her laughter filling the rooms.

Chapter 19
Astrid

A chill ran through me as we walked on the trail to take us to the cliffs. It wasn't a chill of cold but of something deeper. As if the chill was coming from my heart to my bones.

I felt this feeling a few times before when I was hunting with my uncle and father. A feeling that all hunters knew, the feeling of something hunting them.

I experienced this feeling once as a child when I was almost attacked by a rabid wolf. The other time was when I saved Aiden from the hunters that had caught him. My eyes looked at my pups, all asleep and close together in the safety of our wagon.

"Calum," I called, and soon he was beside me.

"I know my lady." He said his only body was ready to fight also.

"I guess I'm not the only one who feels the chill."

"At least 5 other shifters have felt it, and some who share shifter blood can feel it also."

"What do you think it is?"

Calum took a breath, closing his eyes and then opening them a second to reveal the eyes of a hunting bird. Calum looked deep into the woods before us, a frown on his face. I called on my own gift, my senses awaking as smells hit my nose.

The scents of pine and fur filled my nose, but then their smell of iron. Then the sound of heavy footsteps on the land and soft creaking filled the air. I felt myself growl, my instincts calling me to protect my pups and those around me.

"It's a group of soldiers, armed and armored," Calum stated.

"Yeah, and with their smell, they have already taken some lives; even iron scent shouldn't be this strong."

"Astrid?" the voice of Nels entered our conversation, and we turned to the dragon of ice.

"There is a group of soldiers heading this way," I growled.

"Are you sure….never mind, I forget the gifts that shfiters have."

"So what should we do?" Calum asked.

"We need to get the elders and children away from here. Ask those shifters of the Ursa, Finnins, and Maccons' clan to help. They have experience in the woods and will be stronger against those soldiers."

"But they have blades…wouldn't a dragon.."

"Dragons, though their skin is tough, are too big," I replied, looking over at the cart.

"Astrid…"

"Besides, having dragons protect the fledglings is more important."

"You forget the bond between the dragons and their Flares and Flareas."

"Milday is right; our goal is to protect the children. Ask those with elder children to come; if their mate is carrying, or they have babes, they shouldn't come." Calum added his own voice growling.

"I hope that includes our queen."

"I will help; I'm one of the wolves of Finnis."

"You're also the queen and young mother," Nels said, frowning.

"Then how could I ask those shifters to do what if I ask if I don't go myself," I replied.

"Spoken like a child of Finnis." a voice added.

I turned to see a group of shifters; they ranged from my age to 40's summers. Their head was a Ursa shifter with golden blond hair and built like a mountain. His honey-colored eyes from his summers reminded me of my uncle's warmth.

"Thank you…"

"I'm Hallbjorn, the mate of Alma the dragon flames."

"And one of the leaders of the Flares and Flareas of shifter blood," Calum added with a smile.

"You must think me a fool since I had no idea."

"Milady, you have had enough on your plate since you came here. You had your cubs to carry and the weight of the dragons on your mind."

"So you heard us talking…"

"You two aren't the only shifters. So what do you want to do?"

"I was thinking of driving them away, at least until the wagons are safely away from here," I explained.

"We might want one to see what they know," Calum said.

"Why?"

"Because I want to know how they knew about us leaving."

I bit my lip and looked at him, my thoughts following it. Someone had given the enemy our plans; a traitor was in our midst, but the question remained: were they with us or with my mate?

Chapter 20
Emyr

Rinbow, the elfin kingdom, lived up to its name as the kingdom of starlight. The walls caved with magic, which was see-through, but it showed like stars in the night sky when the light hit. A kingdom of light for those made from the stars that took over everything.

"Are you alright, Prince Emyr?" Lord Gael asked, moving to sit beside me.

"Well, I have been asked to forsake my vow to protect all Kardian, was almost killed by a wolf, then by my brother's knights and my best friend is wounded…" I said point blank.

"I am sorry about Freki's overprotectiveness. Just think of it as training for the Elf king; you aren't just the son of the human king and brother of the man who wants to kill everything he loves. You also put one of his grandchildren in danger."

"Does it count that I didn't want any of that?" I asked with a sigh.

"It should, but life isn't always something we can count on or change. Sometimes, our lives aren't our own."

"You're talking about our lives, those of noble blood. I know that we have to live our lives for our families.."

"Not just those of our blood. Even children who are dirt poor have to sometimes live for the sake of others."

"I know.." I replied, gripping my pants. I knew all too well the prices some would go to protect or feed their own bellies.

My master and I had gone to a slave market. He had brought me there to learn a lesson. That people, deep down, had five things that controlled their hearts: love, hatred, sadness, greed, and fear.

One could bring you to the slave market for taking, but more often than not, you would be the one sold. Man's thoughts in their hearts drove them to do things others might deem reckless or vile. Yet even knowing so, they do it because their heart leads them to it.

"I wonder what leads my brother's heart."

"I think the question you should ask Prince Emyr is, what leads yours."

✳✳✳✳✳✳✳

Lord Gael's words echoed in my mind as we walked through the stone walls of the Elfin castle. Ingrid, Freki, and her uncle went first; it looked like they were in their own home. Their voices were loud and filled with laughter, and their bodies showed relaxed curves instead of the sharp angles of fear and anger that I had seen a few days earlier.

Lord Gael and I were after them; unlike the ones in front of us, we seemed to be filled with worry, with goose flesh appearing on both of our skins. I hadn't felt this nervous since the first time I met my master. I had been a child of 9 then and had just gotten the news I was supposed to be a new novice after my master retired.

My thoughts then turned to Willow, who had been taken once we had entered the city. The elf Ash had left with him, saying he would heal my friend. Part of me believed he would, yet another part still worried that he wouldn't be able to because of Willows's blood.

"Please, Solara…help and guide hands to heal my dear friend."

"Be careful who you call in the castle of our king," a voice said behind me.

I didn't look back; I had heard the talk from the guards since we came to the castle. They seemed fine with the shifters and Ingrid, but Lord Gael and myself weren't very welcome. I also knew that they were watching my every move along with Gael; to them, we were the humans who put one of their royal lines in danger.

Soon, we entered the throne room, a place of white stone and sapphire colors. The floor was a cool stone so dark that it matched the night sky. Yet everyone's eyes went to the twin thrones, which took up the center of the room. Pure white, they shone like the stars above. Sitting on these thrones were two elves.

One of the queens dressed in fine silk, which was the color of blue, her golden hair twisted in a bun, and her violet eyes bore into the group before her. Beside her was the elf king, dressed in the same color but with a crown of silver with blue sea stones etched into it.

"Presting the High king of Elves, Orion, and his wife, Queen Astra." a servant called as my eyes went to the king.

"Welcome to my kingdom." the king said, smiling at us all.

"Thank you, sir," Furrow replied as we all bowed.

"Furrow, you don't need to bow to us; you are family, the same as my great-grandchild and the heir of Maccon."

"Thank you, sir," Felki said with a smile.

"Now, the two humans."

"Lord Gael of Mar and Emery, the younger prince of Zodian and the novice of the voice of Solara," Ingrid said, looking from her grandparents to us.

"I have heard of you both, elf friends, to the point that you would risk your own lives, and I know coming here isn't your first choice."

"How…" I found myself asking.

"Our lady has her own voice here. I have also heard some of the voices of Flickron and other minor gods and goddesses. The war has come to our time."

"Yes…"

"And it seems you have a choice to make which will change your life."

"Yes, that's what the Lady of Lace told me."

"So you spoke to her yourself." He said, his eyes looking at me with understanding.

"Yes..she asked me to help."

"And have you made the choice yet?"

I bit my lip; my mind and heart were struggling with that question. Flashes of pain and hurt, the worry and destruction that would come. Yet a part of me was still trying to hold to my old life.

"Enough, it's night, and all of you need rest. Some of the best decisions are made with a good night's rest," Astra called out, her voice like a soft lullaby.

"My wife is right. Besides, there are words to be spoken by my blood."

I watched as Ingrid walked to the queen's arms and left the chamber. The two shifters followed knights following them. Then it was just us and the king; his eyes looked up at us.

"I pray you two have a good night; take them to their rooms."

"Sire, they are human…"

"They have been chosen by the Lady of Lace, and one is a friend of my granddaughter. You will treat them with respect." The king ordered.

"Yes sire."

Then the king left, and we were taken to our rooms. Yet even as we took steps, the cool spring breeze seemed warm. I then looked at Lord Gael, who frowned and gripped his fists.

"Lord Gael?"

"Dragons, but why now?"

"Dragons…"

"Yes, but they should have been in their nests, so why would they come here?"

"Maybe to help."

"But if there here…"

Lord Gael ran, and I didn't know why, but I followed; something had caused him to worry, and I was going to find out why. Little did I know that those steps had sealed my fate.

Chapter 21
Blaggdon

I and other dragons who came with me landed on a patch of grass just outside the palace of the Elves. Part of me knew we should have waited, but something had driven me to get here as soon as possible. I had just transformed into my human form when I heard footsteps and saw a human.

"Lord Gael," I said with a slight mixture of tiredness and annoyance.

"Dragen…" he said with a bow.

Behind him came a boy close to my Flera's age, but with his scent, I knew he was. A novice to a temple, and by how he held himself, he was part of a higher line.

"Lord Gael?" the boy asked.

"Prince Emery, this is Dragen, or king of dragons."

"The king of dragons." He said in awe.

"Yes, and you must be the younger son of the late king."

"How did you…"

"We're dragons; humans make it their business to hunt or hurt us. So it is ideal for us to know what's going on." I replied, my eyes narrowing at him.

"Yes, I suppose you're right. I didn't mean to sound foolish."

"Not foolish; you're just young," Roka said from beside me.

"My advisor is right; you are still young. You still have a lot to learn about the world." I said, my thoughts turning to my own fledglings.

"I do have a question; what brings you here?" Lord Gael asked.

"I was invited; the king wanted me to meet him."

"At night?"

"No, but something told me to get here right away."

"A feeling?" Gael asked, his voice and face turned to a worried frown.

"What is it?" I asked, feeling something off.

"When did you get news about the meeting?"

"A couple of days…"

"Lord Gael?" the prince asked.

"What do I owe the audience with the king of Dragons." A voice from behind Gael said.

I looked at the elfin king, who seemed puzzled at my presence. I quickly reached into my bag and pulled out the letter.

"I was following your summoning."

I gave him the letter and watched as his face furrowed with puzzlement, then a flash of fear before it was replaced with an unreadable frown. He then walked over to me, crumbling the paper as he went.

"For one, I would not send you a message like this. It would be better to hear a message than on paper.

Secondly, it's not my writing. Thirdly, I didn't know where you call home."

"Then how…"

That's when I heard the sound of tiny wings. We all looked up to see a falcon. One of the dragons in my company quickly moved seeing the bird. The said bird, seeing the dragon, flew straight to the dragon, quickly transforming into a small boy.

"Papa."

"Sky, what are you doing here? You were supposed to be with your mama, along with your siblings and the rest." the dragon said. I could hear the fear in his voice.

"There were soldiers…they were following us…" the boy was having a hard time breathing, and his body was shaking.

"Soldiers!?" I asked, walking toward the boy.

"My king please," Roka called.

I took a breath and walked to Sky; the young boy seemed terrified. I knelt down and went to touch the boy when a voice behind me called.

"Please forgive him."

I turned to see the voice, only to feel a pain in my chest. I looked down to see a blade buried deep inside it. The boy had tears in his eyes, but I also saw black markings.

"A curse…" I groaned, touching the boy and breaking it.

"My king." I felt Roka and Elctra run to my side.

"The boy…look at him cursed…"

"We saw. Don't worry, my lord." Roka replied, his hands touching my wound.

"I didn't mean to. They said if I didn't, they would hurt mama…" the boy cried.

"Elctra…" I looked over at her.

She nodded, going over to the dragon and boy, using her magic to comfort him. I smiled at this as sleep called to me.

"My lord, you must stay awake…"

"Roka…please…protect our people…"

"Milord…"

Hold on, king of dragons, she is coming.

"My Flera…I wish…to see…."

"Blaggdon!" a voice like thunder filled the air and winds blew around us.

Chapter 22
Astrid

I was with the shifters, who had also chosen to fight. The plan was to attack the soldiers while the rest of our people headed to the beach. Yet even as we parted, a feeling of fear and worry filled me.

"Milday?" Calum asked from his spot beside me.

"Something is wrong…not just the group of soldiers in front of us."

"I get that feeling too; let's get this done. Then we can head back to the others and your brood."

I nodded before facing the other shifters behind me. We all agreed to fight, but also to be careful not to kill every soldier. We needed at least one alive to figure out who had betrayed the dragons. To aid us in this, we would use Flickron's gift.

Flickron's gift, or fear as some humans called it, was when a shifter let their animal side take over. They become the animal they shifted into, ready to kill and act like that animal. It was a gift that was to be used sparingly because of how much toll it took on a shifter's body and mind. There had been cases where a shifter lost their human part and became the animal of their line.

"Remember, we are going to do this quickly and quietly. They have swords, but we have claws, fangs, and teeth. We need to make sure we don't get hurt."

"Understood." the group chorused.

I nodded and turned back to the front, my body already feeling the twinges of my other form. Soon, winter blond fur covered my body and my wolf came too. Soon, I was surrounded by the smells of other wolves, birds of prey, the bears of the north, and a few other shifters who were from minor families.

We waited until we saw the glimmer of silver; once I saw it, I howled, my voice echoing through the woods around us. My paws barely touched the ground as I attacked. I attacked the first soldier I saw, quickly taking him down as I would with an elk.

After that attack, the air was filled with growls and howls, along with men's screams. We quickly went through them until there was only a handful left. I changed into my human form and walked to the leader.

"Do your worst, dog." the leader growled.

"You better watch your words. Most of the wolves here are older than me, and don't appreciate you talking to their queen or clan mate like that." I replied with a smile.

"Queen...You're the dragon's queen!" he said, his face going pale.

"Yes, and the look on your face tells me that you know about me."

"You're a shifter of the Finnis clan..."

"And the blood of the high elves runs through me, a favorite of both Lady of Lace and Flickron."

I walked closer, reaching for my dagger, walking over to the man. Anger filling me at each step.

"You come to hunt my people down, those who are grandparents and those who are just born not able to fight. You attack those who have no choice or defense."

I place the dagger on his neck.

"Now tell me, should I let you live.."

Queen of Dragons, lower your blade.

I stopped looking at the hand that held mine.

I looked over to the Faia, the goddess of Earth, and my aunt. Her brow was filled with worry and sadness. I let my hand drop as the goddess then helped me up.

"Lady Faia…"

These men will pay for their crimes, but you have something important to do. I'm afraid you must go, my dear. for time is short.

"What do you mean…"

Calum, child of the winds, come here.

Calum quickly ran over to the goddess and me. He quickly bowed as Faia nodded to him.

You are charged not just in guiding and protecting the young ones with you but also in protecting those of the king of dragons, and you are blessed by the Lady of Lace and Flickron. You will protect and guide them to the shores of the North. Your queen will follow you later.

"If I may…"

You are a child blessed by your family, though you have no children. You treat the queen as your sister; her young are your blood. Protect them, for their mother is needed here.

"Faia…" my voice filled with fear, my heart thumping.

Take my gift, dear; go to your king. He needs you.

I watched as the wind picked up and Tempest, the horse of the wind, appeared. The gift from my aunt on the day of marriage. I hadn't ridden him once, but I found myself jumping and landing on his back as he walked toward me.

"I…" I said, looking at the shifters.

"Go, my lady, if it were any of our mates, we would be at their side." One of the shifter women said with a smile.

"Thank you."

I then left, winds and thunder following after as if it were to match my heart. I could feel the sting of tears in my eyes; I didn't know if it was the rain or my tears. Soon, I was in a familiar courtyard, but my memories of happiness were shattered when I saw my mate lying with a dagger in his chest.

"Blaggdon!"

Chapter 23
Emyr

My heart broke at the scene before me. A woman ran to the king, and the way that she pulled him into her arms, I knew for a fact that she was his mate. Yet when I got a good look at her, my eyes widened; her looks reminded me only of one person.

"She's…"

"Astrid, the sister of Ingrid and the wife of the Dragen." Lord Gael whispered to me.

"Ingrid's sister…but does that mean that she is the child of the…."

Astrid is my daughter by blood, the one that came from my mates and I love. A voice whispered in my ear.

"Lady of Lace.." I said, turning and saw the Lady of Lace dressed in a simple dress.

She gave me a small nod before walking over to the couple. As she walked, I could feel the air around us thicken as if a storm would rage. I looked at Lord Gael, who was softly whispering something, and that's when I realized it was prayer.

It wasn't one that I had heard before, but another voice filled my ears. This one was a mixture of tiredness and anger; I looked up to see a shifter with fox-like eyes.

"He's calling forth the peace from Asha, the goddess of peace."

"A minor goddess…"

"But still, your father understood that all gods and goddesses are important to the people who believe in them. Also, your master."

"You're Flickron."

"Yes, now forgive me, prince, I need to go to my daughter."

I watched the scene as the two gods saw their daughter holding her mate in her hands. Like trees standing against a harsh wind, they bent but didn't break. At least not until they were needed.

"Brother…does your hate go so far as to sadden gods.." I said to myself.

I then thought that Willow was also hurt protecting me from my brother's hate. The Lady of Lace's words echoed in my heart again.

"I made my choice."

"Sire?" Lord Gael.

"I will fight against my brother. I will save Kardian."

Chapter 24
Blaggdon

"Blaggdon, please." I heard my love's voice as warm arms led me to lap.

"You are supposed to be with the Fledgins…on your way to the North."

"Your people and pups are safe; Faia has taken them."

"The Goddess of Earth loves her blood, I see."

"You will find that she also wanted to protect her blood." I heard her reply as I felt wetness on my forehead.

"I'm sorry that you have seen me like this.."

"Don't say that; it's my fault. I shouldn't have left you."

"You are my queen, not just my mate. I couldn't let you be in danger." I replied, reaching up to wipe away her tears.

"But you were…"

"I'm the king and your mate; it's my job."

"Not by yourself…"

"Astrid…"

"Hush, let us heal you…"

"Astrid, this is a blessed blade." I heard a voice answer.

"So, my father-in-law has come to see me off?" I asked with a smirk.

"Blaggdon." I heard Astrid start.

"It's alright; it's not time for things to be kept. Besides, I'm proud of who you are." I told her, smiling.

"Then don't leave me." I could feel magic push against me.

"Astrid, no." I heard a voice that sounded like a harp.

"The Lady of Lace…." I whispered.

"I want to thank you, Dragen, for protecting my daughter and giving me grandchildren."

"Why can't I heal him?" I heard Astrid ask her.

"Because I belong to the Shadowlands, I have for a while now."

"What do…that night when you said you needed to walk, you were in pain."

"I'm sorry, Astrid…"

"Don't say that…please don't…" I watched as her tears came down quickly.

"I would do anything to keep my promise, to see you all safe again."

"Blaggdon…"

"Please….let me kiss my Flarea one more time." I pleaded.

I then felt the warmth of a kiss, filled with love and worry. I gave it an answer filled with my love to comfort her, a last gift before the shadows of death came to me.

"I love you.." I whispered, closing my eyes, lying in the arms of my love.

Chapter 25
Astrid

"No.." I said as I watched my love leave me for the second time.

"Astrid…" I heard the Lady of the Lace start.

"Wasn't it my fate to wed the king of Dragons to save them from death? To be with him for the rest of my life? Wasn't that what you two promised the first king?" I growled at them.

"That is what we promised, but even we can't change what men decide to do." Flickron said.

"No, but you could have stopped it; you could have pulled a trick that you're known for. Or maybe weave a new path for him."

"We couldn't do that; death belongs to Erembour. Only he can decide who lives and dies."

"Then let me talk to him…"

"No. That is one thing I will not let you do." Flickron growled, his body tightening.

"Flickron…"

"No, our child will not go anywhere near the man. His touch can kill anyone or anything. I will not have her near him."

"But everyone goes to him.." I whispered.

"But not you, at least not yet," he said, a protective growl in his voice.

I couldn't help but give him a sad smile.

"Even the best father can't stop death.."

"No, but a child shouldn't be taken from them either."

I looked at Roka, whose amber eyes bore into me with understanding and heartache. Roka had known the feeling of losing his Flarea and one of his children. I quickly bowed my head.

"I'm sorry."

"No, milady, we are the ones who are sorry; we were to protect our king but have failed," Electra added, bowing to me.

I watched as the other dragons followed, and a small boy approached me. His whole body shook as tears flowed from his eyes.

"I'm sorry…I didn't mean it…"

"I know you didn't. You are a child. The one who told you to do it is the one responsible." I said, gently touching his face.

"But I killed him…"

"No, Sky, you did not. The king told you that, right? So never let yourself fall into that." I replied gently, giving him a smile.

"Milday…" Roka then called me back to him.

"Yes."

"We need to get you out of this rain; it's not good for you."

"But.." I looked down at my love.

"I will look after him, Milday; I swear on my fire that he will come to no harm," Electra replied.

I nodded, allowing Roka to help me stand up. I didn't even notice the rain until he said something about it. As we walked, I felt something warm around my shoulders; I looked up to see my father.

"You looked cold."

"Thank you," I whispered.

"Take care of our daughter, Roka, child of Renji."

"I'm a healer, Lord Flickron; it's my job to heal and protect those who need it."

I spared a last look at my love as we entered the halls of Elf Palace. Even though it once filled me with joy

Whittney Corum

and happiness, today, I only felt sadness and loss. A place of warm now cold as the feeling in my heart.

Chapter 26
Emyr

This was the second time that I was to see a king buried. Yet this time, it seemed more profound. Dragons surrounded the body of their fallen king as the king's wife walked over to the pyre.

Even the elves who had come out were dressed in simple garments of soft gray or black. The voices add to the dragons in their own prayer. I followed with my own whispering for the spirit of the king to find peace.

I watched as the queen of Dragons gave a kiss before walking away to the arms of Ingrid and her uncle Furrow, who held both of the women in his arms. Then came the flames from the dragons. As they hit the fire, it burned, taking the body of the king with it.

"Please rest."

"He will, as soon as this war is over." I turned to see the Lady of Lace.

"Lady Lace."

"I heard you made your choice."

"Yes. I want to stop this before more get hurt."

"Good, for I don't think I can ask my daughter for more. Not now."

"Because of her loss."

"Partly, the other is the hope she carries."

"But I thought…" I heard the dragons talking about the three young fledglings that belonged to the royal couple.

"Emyr, even you know how love works. Sometimes, it gives you a gift you didn't know you needed."

"So what will happen?"

"Electra will lead the dragons, while the queen will return to her people."

"But…"

"She is following her parents' and husband's wishes."

"Won't they say that she is weak?"

"You mean because she will leave while most of her people stay to fight. No, for them, they knew the decision to make. The queen and her children, along with those waiting on the ships, will take the path North to find safety."

"While those who stay will fight to protect them."

"Yes, and soon elves and shifters will follow suit; those who want will leave Kardian to the lands of their home or places of friendship."

"But what of humans?" I found myself asking.

"That I cannot answer. You are the one who chose to protect and save this land as a human. It's up to you, Prince Emyr. You're the one who has to face your father's folly."

"His folly? You mean my brother and his wife. He thought it would help them both.."

"I know, and your father was a great king, but even kings can make mistakes and fall like any man."

"Then how do I know if I would make the same mistakes as him?"

"You asking that question is a step in the right direction. Shine like the morning start, Prince Emyr. May you take the throne in peace."

"Thank you, Lady of Lace, and may my song of old bring you happiness and life."

I then felt the wind whip around me before everything was quiet. The Lady was right, though; my father had made mistakes like his own, and now my brother. I would make mistakes too, but I knew in my heart one thing that I would use mine to fix my father's folly.

The End

Lunar series book 3: King's Folly

Whittney Corum

Lunar series book 3: King's Folly

Whittney Corum

Made in the USA
Columbia, SC
19 June 2024